A Note for Parents and Teachers

A focus on phonics helps beginning readers gain
skill and confidence with reading. Each story in the
Bright Owl Books series highlights one vowel sound—
for *Hop, Frog!*, it's the short "o" sound. At the end of
the book, you'll find two Story Starters, just for fun.
Story Starters are open-ended questions that can be
used as a jumping-off place for conversation,
storytelling, and imaginative writing.

At Kane Press, we believe the most important part of
any reading program is the shared experience
of a good story. We hope you'll enjoy
Hop, Frog! with a child you love!

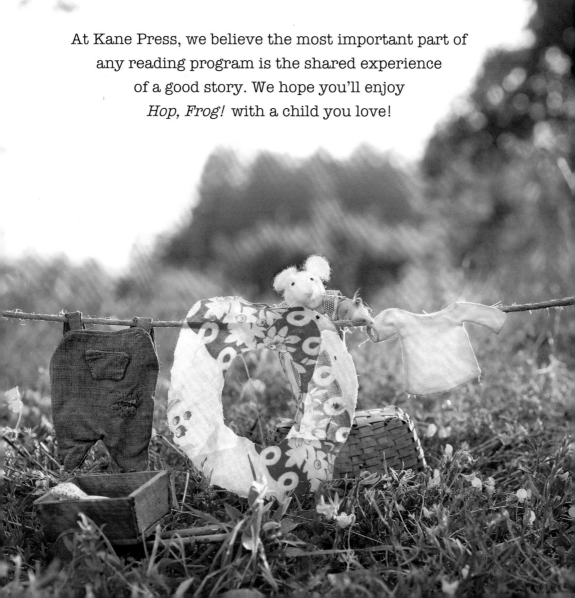

Library of Congress Cataloging-in-Publication Data
Names: Coxe, Molly, author, illustrator.
Title: Hop, frog! / by Molly Coxe.
Description: First Kane Press edition. | New York : Kane Press, [2018] |
Series: Bright owl books | Summary: "Frog helps the other animals in the hopping contest until he needs some help himself in this easy-to-read featuring the short 'o' sound"—Provided by publisher.
Identifiers: LCCN 2017054185| ISBN 9781575659824 (pbk) | ISBN 9781575659817 (reinforced library binding) | ISBN 9781575659831 (ebook)
Subjects: | CYAC: Stories in rhyme. | Frogs—Fiction. | Helpfulness—Fiction. | Animals—Fiction.
Classification: LCC PZ8.3.C8395 Hm 2018 | DDC [E]—dc23
LC record available at https://lccn.loc.gov/2017054185

10 9 8 7 6 5 4 3 2 1

Printed in China

Book Design: Michelle Martinez

Bright Owl Books is a trademark of Kane Press, Inc.

Visit us online at
www.kanepress.com

Like us on Facebook
facebook.com/kanepress

Follow us on Twitter
@KanePress

HOP, Frog!

by Molly Coxe

Kane Press • New York

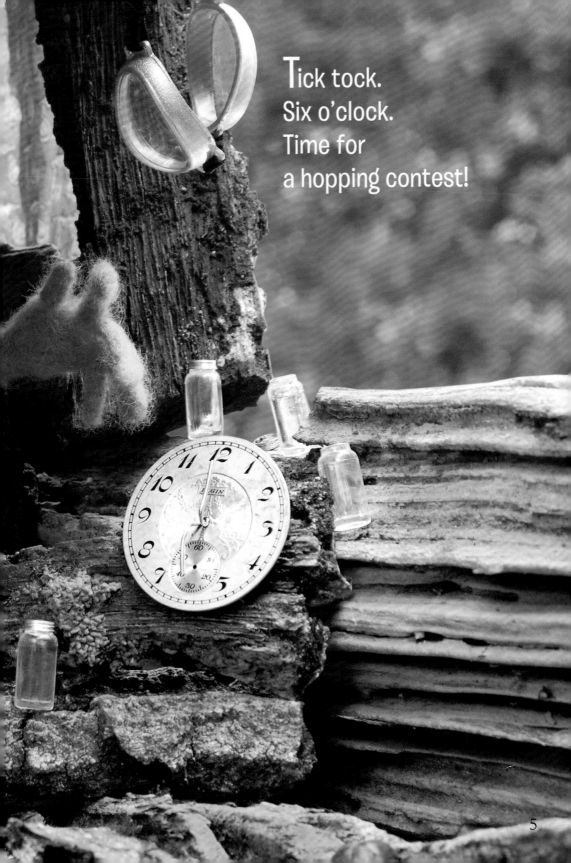

Tick tock.
Six o'clock.
Time for
a hopping contest!

Ready, set, **hop!**

Frog hops.

Frog stops.
He helps Pollywog
onto a log.

"Thanks, Frog!" says Pollywog.
"No problem!" says Frog.

Frog hops.

Frog stops.
He helps Fox
out of a bog.

17

"Thanks, Frog!" says Fox.
"No problem!" says Frog.

Frog hops.

Frog stops.
He helps Ox
off a rock.

"Thanks, Frog!" says Ox.
"No problem!" says Frog.

Frog hops.

Frog stops.

Frog drops!
"Frog is hot!" shouts Pollywog.
"Too hot to hop!"

Ox, Fox, and Pollywog
cross the line
with Frog.

"Who won?" asks Frog.
Everyone!

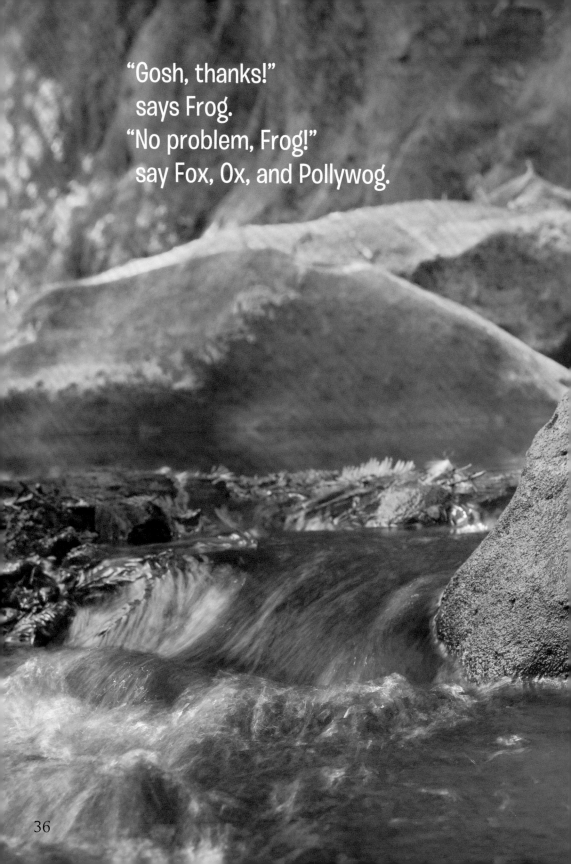

"Gosh, thanks!"
says Frog.
"No problem, Frog!"
say Fox, Ox, and Pollywog.

Story Starters

Pollywog is on a log.
Where will she go?

What do Mom and Tom
see in the fog?